To Patty Saccente, my dear friend,
without whom not much would be possible
— B.P.

To Jack and Alessandra Lynn St. Ledger—
for your precious hearts and creative minds
— L.M.

A BROADWAY BARKS™ BOOK

All author royalties from this book will be donated to Broadway Barks,
a program that promotes the adoption of shelter animals.

Text copyright © 2015 by Bernadette Peters
Illustrations copyright © 2015 by Liz Murphy
All rights reserved / CIP data is available.
Published in the United States 2015 by
Blue Apple Books, 515 Valley Street, Maplewood, NJ 07040
www.blueapplebooks.com

First Edition
07/15
Printed in China

ISBN: 978-1-60905-535-6

2 4 6 8 10 9 7 5 3 1

Bernadette Peters

Stella and Charlie: Friends Forever

paintings by Liz Murphy

BLUE 🍎 APPLE

Stella lived in an apartment
in New York City with her
best friend, Kramer.
One day he was gone—
and Stella was alone.

Stella didn't want to play with her toys.

She refused her favorite meatballs.

But worst of all, she did not want
to dance anymore.
(Oh, yes…Stella was a dancing dog!)

She just waited by the door for her friend to come back.

But Kramer was not coming home.
Stella's mom wanted to find her a new friend.

So she decided she would adopt another dog.

She looked at many pictures of dogs who needed homes.
She checked out dogs at animal shelters.
But she couldn't find just the right friend for Stella.

Finally, she heard about a little brown dog,
who was found in a garbage dumpster.

A lady heard the frightened puppy's cries and rescued him.

The dog, who answered to the name Charlie,
was taken to an animal shelter in Texas.

And Stella's mom was in New York,
two thousand miles away.

But because her dog really needed a friend, Stella's mom decided it might be worth driving to Texas to meet Charlie.

She waved good-bye to Stella, and off she went.

When Stella's mom met Charlie, he wrapped himself
around her as if to say, "Yes, I have been waiting for you."

Charlie looked at her with his big black eyes.
She talked to him. And he listened.
She sang to him. And he sang back.

Yes, this little dog could actually sing.
What a perfect match
for Stella!

And so...
Charlie was adopted!

Off they went on a three-day road trip—

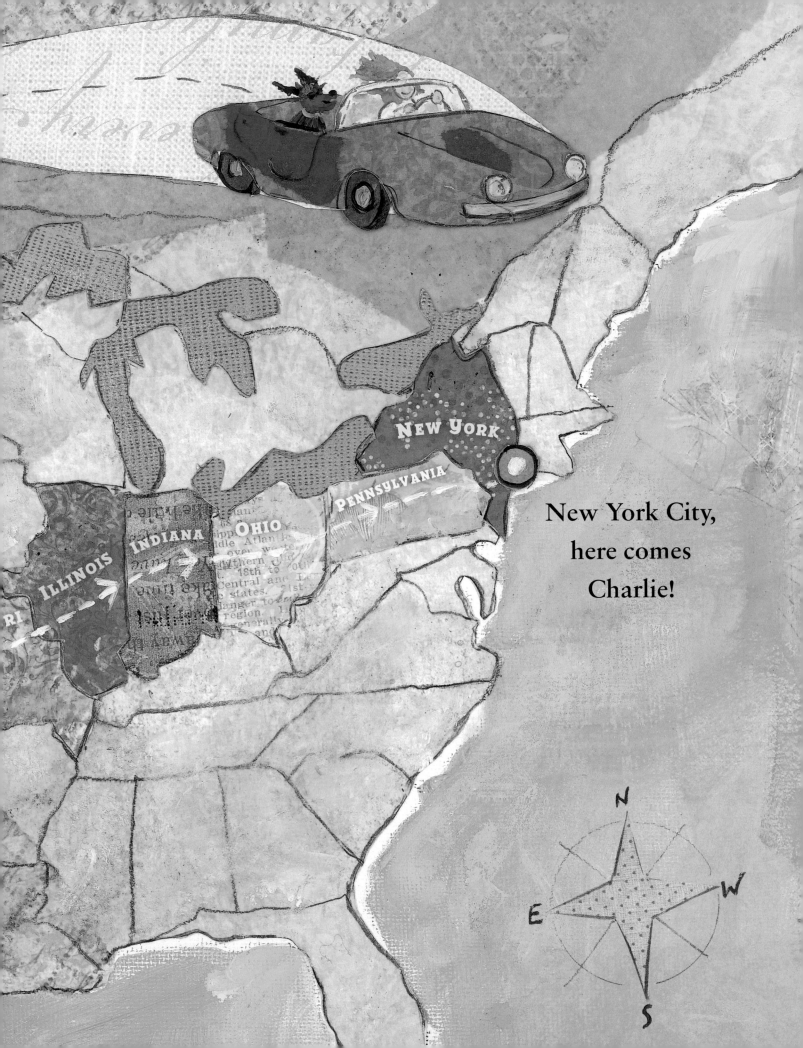

New York City,
here comes
Charlie!

Charlie spent his first night in a hotel in Missouri.
He had a plain hot dog from room service for
dinner. No mustard, please!

Charlie was so happy he did
a little "thank you" yodel.

The next day, they were
on their way again.
"Let's go, Charlie. It's going
to be a long drive."

They sang as they drove through Missouri on their way to Indiana.

Charlie became car sick.
Yuck!

They stopped for a while so he could go for a walk.

The sun shining on
the Gateway Arch
made a rainbow of color.
This made Charlie
feel much better.

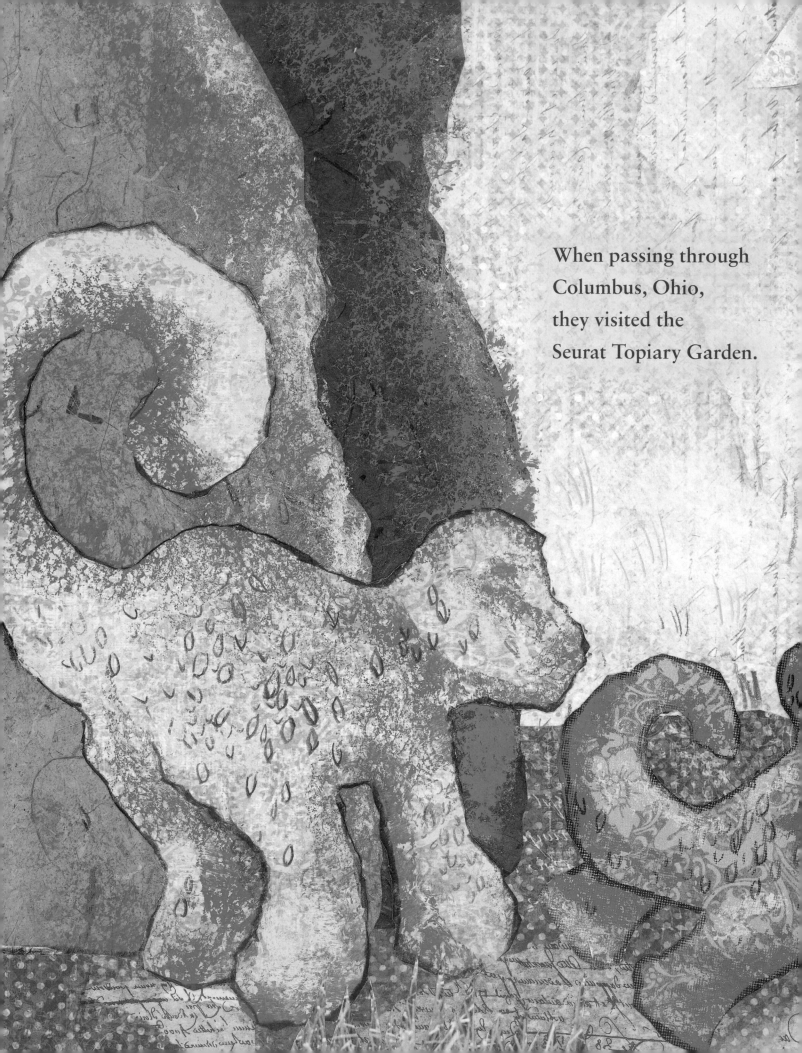

When passing through
Columbus, Ohio,
they visited the
Seurat Topiary Garden.

Charlie smelled everything
in the garden. Delicious!

He liked the dog.
But his favorite sculpture was the monkey.

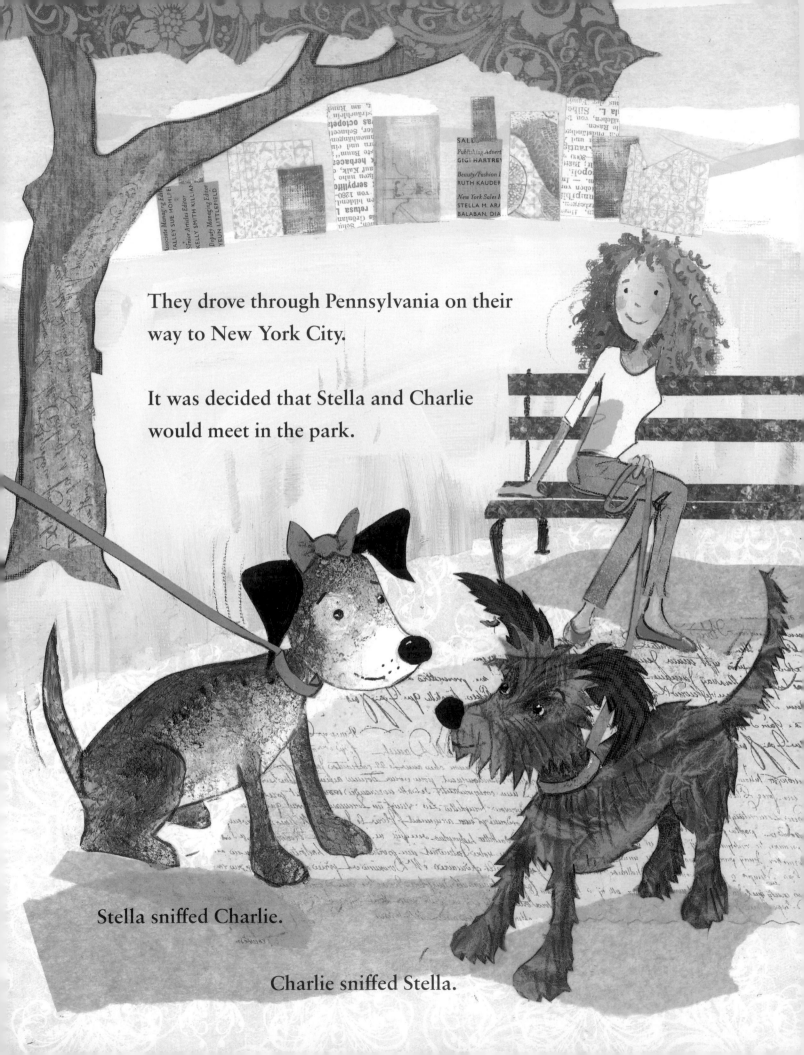

They drove through Pennsylvania on their way to New York City.

It was decided that Stella and Charlie would meet in the park.

Stella sniffed Charlie.

Charlie sniffed Stella.

Stella chased Charlie. Charlie chased Stella.

They jumped... they ran... they played.

Then Stella led
Charlie home.
She knew the way!

Stella wanted to play and show Charlie around, but he wasn't interested.
He preferred being held and kissed.

It took a few days before
Charlie was comfortable in his new home.
Stella taught him the rules.

Don't jump
on guests.

Always eat
in the kitchen.

No chewing
on the chairs...

and don't piddle
on the floor!

After a few weeks, Stella realized—

Charlie was playing with HER toys...

and sleeping in HER bed...

and hugging HER mom...

and licking HER bowl—
sometimes even before
she had finished eating!

Stella wanted a friend.
But she didn't want to share.
Not her toys.
Not her food.
But most of all, NOT her MOM!

One day in the park,
a bumblebee stung Stella
on the nose.

Ouch!

When Stella came home, she went right to her bed.

Charlie came over
and licked the sore spot
on her nose.

You know what?
It made it feel better!

Then Charlie brought Stella
one of his toys,
and Stella gave him a kiss.

Later, when the two
of them played together,
Stella shared her toys.
She even allowed Charlie
to lick her bowl.

On rainy days when they could not go to the park,
Mom sang and played the piano.

Stella danced.
And Charlie yodeled!

Stella had a forever friend,
and Charlie had a forever home.